THE
TORTOISE
AND THE
DARE

by Terry Deary

illustrated by Helen Flook

PICTURE WINDOW BOOKS
Minneapolis, Minnesota

Editor: Shelly Lyons
Page Production: Michelle Biedscheid
Art Director: Nathan Gassman
Associate Managing Editor: Christianne Jones

First American edition published in 2008 by
Picture Window Books
5115 Excelsior Boulevard
Suite 232
Minneapolis, MN 55416
877-845-8392
www.picturewindowbooks.com

First published in 2007 by A&C Black Publishers Limited, 38 Soho Square,
London W1D 3HB, with the title THE TORTOISE AND THE DARE.

Printed in the United States of America.

Library of Congress Cataloging-in-Publication Data
Deary, Terry.
The tortoise and the dare / by Terry Deary ; illustrated by Helen
Flook — 1st American ed.
p. cm. — (Read-it! chapter books) (Historical tales)
Summary: Furious that her twin brother, Cypselis, promised her as a
slave should he lose a footrace, Ellie must find a way for tortoise-slow
Cypselis to beat his classmate to the finish line at their school in
ancient Greece. Includes facts about the Olympic Games.
ISBN-13: 978-1-4048-4051-5 (library binding)
[1. Racing—Fiction. 2. Brothers and sisters—Fiction.
3. Twins—Fiction. 4. Wagers—Fiction. 5. Sportsmanship—Fiction.
6. Greece—History—To 146 B.C.—Fiction.] I. Flook, Helen, ill.
II. Title.
PZ7.D3517Tor 2008
[Fic]—dc22   2007035612

Table of Contents

Words to Know

Aesop—a Greek storyteller whose fables teach a lesson

Heracles—one of the greatest heroes among the Greek gods; he was known for his strength, courage, and wit

Olympia—the place in Ancient Greece where the Olympic Games were first held

Pelops—the grandson of the Greek god Zeus; his father sacrificed him to the gods

quoit—a flattened ring of iron or circle of rope

Chapter One

In the Beginning

Olympia, Greece, 776 B.C.

Aesop the Greek storyteller said:
Slow and steady wins the race.

It started with the mighty Heracles, the hero of the gods. Heracles won a race at Olympia, the home of the gods. Well, he could easily win a race—he was the strongest, fastest hero the world has ever known. I think he was like a lot of people. He was vain.

"The world must remember my great victory," Heracles said. "Humans must have races every four years! They will be called the Olympics."

The men agreed. And that's how the Olympic Games began.

But Heracles didn't just start the Olympic Games. He also started a lot of trouble.

A lot of people enjoy watching the Olympic Games. They love the show, the sports, and the excitement. But what about the losers? What about the cheating? What about arguments? And what about the women?

Women are not allowed to race, of course. They are not even allowed to watch. If they try to watch the race, they are executed—thrown from a cliff!

Ooooh! It makes me so angry. I am an angry sort of person. I was angry when I was a girl, all of those years ago, and I am still angry today.

I am angry with my brother, Cypselis. He had a bet on a race that he would run. And what was the prize? Me! Yes, he bet his own sister!

Would you do that? No, of course not. So, do not blame me for being angry now, when I tell you the tale of "The Tortoise and the Dare."

The Bet

My brother, Cypselis, ran in from school, bubbling like a soup pot. He was so happy that he didn't notice how miserable the rest of the family was.

"The Olympic Games start next week, and our head teacher, Master Sophos, said we can have our own school Olympics tomorrow," Cypselis told us. He turned to me and continued, "Ellie, there will be all sorts of prizes, and it will be more exciting than the real Olympic Games."

"Nice," I muttered.

"The boys at school have already started talking about who will win. We're doing the same events as the real Olympians. There's the foot race, which is 200 paces, and the double foot race, which is 400 paces. We'll have the standing long jump, quoit throwing, and javelin!" he said.

"Great," I said.

"I think I could win the foot race," Cypselis said. "I'll practice after dinner. Are we having cheese and milk?"

"Bread and water," Mother sighed.

"But I love cheese and milk!" Cypselis protested loudly.

"Bread and water," I said, louder.

Cypselis blinked and replied, "An athlete needs cheese and milk."

"Where will we get it from?" I snapped back at him.

Cypselis laughed and said, "Why, from Nan the goat, of course."

Father told him, "They came and took Nan away from us today."

"Who did?" asked Cypselis.

"The priests from the temple. They hold a feast before the Olympic Games start. They will sacrifice 20 goats to Pelops. They took Nan to sacrifice."

"Then what will I eat?" Cypselis cried to us all.

That's when I lost my temper and screamed, "Oh, don't worry about poor Nan. Don't worry about Mother and Father getting through the winter. And don't worry about finding the money for another goat. All you can think about is your stomach!"

Cypselis blushed. He wasn't really thoughtless, just stupid. He nodded. "Sorry, Ellie," he muttered.

"You deserve to be sacrificed like Pelops!" I raged.

"Maybe I can win a goat if I win the race," he said quietly.

I stopped shouting and listened. "A goat is the prize?" I asked.

"Not exactly," Cypselis replied. "I have a dare with Big Bacchiad, a boy in my class. He said he will give me a goat if I can beat him."

I frowned. "And what will you give him if *he* beats *you*?" I asked.

Cypselis muttered something.

"What did you say?" I asked.

He looked up with a smile and said, "I told him he could have you as his slave, Ellie."

That's when I started hitting him.

"I'm sorry!" Cypselis bellowed. "Mother, don't let her hit me! Mother! Oh, ouch!"

Chapter Three

The Practice Run

I know you think I will say I lost my temper again, but I didn't.

I felt sick with fear. When two men make a bargain, it must be kept. A dare between two young boys is just as strong.

Cypselis had bet me against a goat. If he lost the race, I would be given away as a slave. There was nothing I could do to stop it now.

In Greece, a woman is treated as if she is worthless. Women are just there to do what men tell them to do.

Our mother groaned. "Cypselis!" she said. "Ellie is your twin sister. You shouldn't have treated her like that."

"But I will win," my brother said bravely. "By this time tomorrow, we will have a new goat!"

I began to say, "But if you lose—"

"I won't!" he quickly replied.

I stood up. "Let's see you run, then," I said.

I knew how fast my brother was. We used to race by the river every day when we were young—before Cypselis started going to school.

He was fast. But I was faster.

We set off across the fields, and as fast as he ran, I was quicker. We climbed a small hill. I reached the top a few paces ahead of him.

The evening sun was low in the sky and the earth was still warm as we lay on the ground, panting.

"You're a tortoise compared to me, Cypselis," I said. "A tortoise!"

I looked down into the valley. The
stadium stood there with its high walls
casting long shadows over the track.
Some boys were there, racing around
the course.

"There's Big Bacchiad," Cypselis said,
and he pointed at the boy in the lead.

Bacchiad was tall and powerful. He was the son of Olympia's richest farmer. And he had the strength of one of his father's bulls.

"Let's see how fast he is," I said. I got up and trotted down the hill ahead of Cypselis.

In the stadium, Big Bacchiad was sweating, but he was pleased with himself. He saw Cypselis and laughed aloud. "I've beaten everyone, Cypselis. And tomorrow I'll beat you," he said.

"You couldn't even beat his sister," I jeered.

The laughter died in Bacchiad's throat. "And who are you to say that?" he asked.

"His sister," I said and smiled sweetly.

"My prize," he said. "When I win, you will work until you drop." His dark eyes glittered in his ugly face. "You will rise with the sun and gather wood for the fire. You will fetch water from the well and cook breakfast. You will weed in the fields until dark and then—"

"You haven't won me yet," I said.

"But I will," he replied.

"Like I said, you couldn't even race me and win. And Cypselis is faster than me," I lied.

Big Bacchiad looked around the group of boys. "Want to see me race a girl?" he asked.

The boys nodded.

He pointed to one of the boys and ordered, "Then you be the starter, Telemachus. We'll race the length of the stadium, turn at the pillar, and then run back."

"Take your marks!" Telemachus shouted loudly.

Chapter Four

The Secret Plan

"Go!" Telemachus cried.

We set off down the track with the low sun shining in our faces.

Big Bacchiad made the earth shake with his heavy legs. I floated alongside him like a butterfly.

I had speed, but he had strength. When we reached the pillar that marked the turning point, we were shoulder to shoulder.

Bacchiad took a step to the side and jabbed me with his elbow. He turned first and was five paces ahead of me before I recovered.

I was angry. He brought out the worst of my temper. I made my arms pump like a sparrow's wings. I caught up with him before we were halfway down the home stretch.

He saw my shadow next to him, so he swayed and pushed me aside.

This time I was ready for him. I skipped to his left and passed him on the inside.

There were 30 paces left to run. I had the speed. But did I have the strength? With 20 paces to go, Big Bacchiad was alongside me again. He was grunting with the effort.

Every pace took him farther into the lead. When he passed the finish line, he was well ahead of me.

He sank to the ground, shaking with pain, and forced a grin. "You are quite good, girl," he admitted. "But your brother will have to be better if he wants to beat me."

As I walked home with Cypselis, my brother hung his head. "Big Bacchiad beat you, and you are faster than I am. I am going to lose that race," he said.

I smiled. "That's what Bacchiad thinks," I said.

"He beat you," Cypselis repeated.

"I slowed down. I could have beaten him by the length of a goat," I said.

"But you can beat me by the length of two goats. Big Bacchiad will still win tomorrow," Cypselis groaned.

"I know," I said. "You will lose."

"Sorry, Ellie," he said. "I don't think there is a way out of it."

"There is," I said.

Cypselis stopped and looked at me in the half-dark to see if I was joking. "How?" he asked.

"Don't race," I replied.

"But if I refuse to race, Big Bacchiad will claim you as his prize anyway," Cypselis answered.

"I will race him," I said simply. "We are twins. Tonight I will get Mother to cut my hair as short as yours. No one will be able to tell us apart!"

"You're proud of your hair, Ellie," he said. "You'd give it up for me?"

"No," I snapped. "I'll be giving it up for my freedom. Now, let's get home and start cutting."

Chapter Five

The Race

The school Olympics were set to start
in the morning, before the day grew
too hot. Every boy and master in the
school was there, as well as some of the
boys' fathers.

Some young men from the real Olympics were there. Their muscles were shiny and as hard as brass, and they strutted like peacocks to their seats near the finish line.

There were no women there, of course. I was dressed in Cypselis' tunic, and my short hair felt odd.

Big Bacchiad looked at me. "Hello, Cypselis," he sneered. His fat face was bulging as he chewed on some leaves.

I hadn't eaten breakfast. We had no goat and no food.

Big Bacchiad didn't suspect a thing. My twin brother wore a hood, so no one would notice the switch.

Cypselis walked into the arena with me. "Watch out for him at the turn," he said. "He'll try to push you."

I kept my temper and answered, "I know. I raced against him last night. But I might be ahead of him at the turn, and then he won't be able to elbow me."

"The other boys may get in your way," Cypselis said. "Some of them are very fast. But only Big Bacchiad can keep going the full distance."

"I can run the full distance, too," I said.

"Yes, you can, Ellie," Cypselis answered.

Then, the head teacher, Master Sophos, marched onto the starter's platform and clapped his hands. Everyone fell silent.

"Remember, these games must be played in the spirit of the Olympic Games," he announced. "The most important thing is not winning but taking part; the great thing is not winning but competing well. Let us have no cheating, boys!"

He nodded to the bronzed men in the stands and said, "Let us show our heroes that we, too, can be heroes! May the best boy win!"

"Or the best girl," I said to myself. The crowd cheered. The athletes began dividing into two groups—the javelin throwers and the runners.

Master Sophos turned to us and said, "Now, boys, remove your clothes for the race!"

The boys started to slip their tunics over their heads.

I turned to Cypselis. "Why are they taking their clothes off?" I asked.

"Olympians always run naked.
Didn't you know that?" asked Cypselis.

"How *could* I know?" I hissed. "Girls
aren't allowed to watch the Olympic
Games, are they?"

"They won't let you run in a tunic," my brother said as he shrugged.

"Well, I can't take it off or they'll know I'm not a boy!" I replied. "Didn't you think of that?"

Cypselis shrugged again. "I thought you knew," he said. "I thought you'd come up with a way around it."

For once in my life, even my wild temper couldn't find any words to answer him.

I tore Cypselis' hood and tunic off of him and quickly put the hood over my own head.

"Run, tortoise, run," I whispered. Then I hurried off to find a seat in the crowded stands.

Chapter Six

A Strong Finish

My brother tried. At the turn, he was
level with Big Bacchiad. The rest of the
runners were already lengths behind.

Big Bacchiad leaned toward Cypselis and tried to jab him with his shoulder. Cypselis skipped aside, and Bacchiad missed. Bacchiad stumbled and went around the turn with his arms whirling, trying to keep his balance.

By the time they were halfway to the finish line, Cypselis was lengths ahead, but his head was rolling from side to side. I knew it meant he was exhausted. His legs were shaking, and his ankles looked weak.

I thought I could hear Bacchiad's pounding feet above the shouts of the crowd. Every stride took him closer to my brother. Every step took my brother closer to the finish line. My tortoise brother had never run so bravely. Tears filled my eyes, and I screamed until my throat was raw.

But his weary legs stumbled, and
Bacchiad pounded past him just before
they reached the finish line.

A man in a long cloak ran from the
stands and wrapped his arms around
Big Bacchiad.

The man pushed some leaves into Bacchiad's hands, and Bacchiad chewed on them hungrily. The man was Bacchiad's father. He raised his son's arms above his head in victory as Cypselis sank to the ground in despair.

I left the stands and walked over to my brother. I wrapped an arm around him just as Master Sophos stepped down from the starter's platform.

Bacchiad's father was grinning like a wolf. He reached out a hand to take the winner's crown of celery leaves from the head teacher.

But Master Sophos spoke sharply. "You have just given your son some leaves to eat. He was eating them before the race, too."

"Celery," the father said.

Master Sophos stretched out a hand and took a piece from Bacchiad.

He rubbed it and sniffed at the juice he had squeezed out. "It's not celery. It is the candle wort plant," he said.

"So?" asked Bacchiad.

"Athletes know that if they eat the candle wort plant, it makes them run faster for awhile," replied Sophos. "It is banned. It is cheating."

"There's no harm in it!" Bacchiad's father huffed.

"The most important thing in the Olympic Games is not winning but competing well," Sophos said. "Bacchiad has run an unfair race. So, he did not compete well."

The head teacher stepped back onto the platform and held his hands for silence. "Bacchiad has cheated!" he proclaimed. "He loses the race. I now declare the winner to be Cypselis!"

My brother looked in wonder as the wreath was placed on his head. The crowd cheered until their throats were as sore as mine.

That night, my brother showed our father the crown. They were pleased.

I showed Mother something far more precious—the goat.

That night we ate well. Mother raised a glass of milk in a toast to us and said, "Remember, children, the great thing in life is not winning but *eating* well!"

Afterword

The first modern Olympic Games took place in 1896 in Athens, Greece. There were just 241 people who took part. Today, people from all over the world take part in the Olympics. At the 2004 Olympic Games in Athens, there were 11,100 participants from 202 countries.

The modern Olympic Games are modeled after the Ancient Greek Olympics of nearly 3,000 years ago. The legends say the Greek god Heracles marched in a straight line for 400 paces. He said that was how far the runners had to race. Today, running tracks are still 400 meters long.

The Ancient Greek winners didn't get gold, silver, and bronze medals like the modern winners do. The Ancient Greeks were given a crown of olive leaves, because the olive branch is a sign of hope and peace.

But where there are prizes, there are cheaters. No one in Ancient Greece really tried to cheat by putting a girl in place of a boy, as in this story. That would have been too tricky.

Greek cheaters were fined. In fact, there were so many cheaters that the money collected from the fines was enough to build a massive statue of the Greek god Zeus.

On the Web

FactHound offers a safe, fun way to find Web sites related to topics in this book. All of the sites on FactHound have been researched by our staff.

1. Visit *www.facthound.com*
2. Type in this special code:
   1404840516
3. Click on the FETCH IT button.

Your trusty FactHound will fetch the best sites for you!

Look for more *Read-It!* Reader Chapter Books: Historical Tales:

The Actor, the Rebel, and the Wrinkled Queen

The Blue Stone Plot

The Boy Who Cried Horse

The Gold in the Grave

The Lion's Slave

The Magic and the Mummy

The Maid, the Witch, and the Cruel Queen

The Phantom and the Fisherman

The Plot on the Pyramid

The Prince, the Cook, and the Cunning King

The Secret Warning

The Shepherd and the Racehorse

The Thief, the Fool, and the Big Fat King

The Torchbearer

The Tortoise and the Dare

The Town Mouse and the Spartan House